THREE BILLY GOATS GRUFF

For Patricia Rounds, the mother of my granddaughters, with much love

Library of Congress Cataloging-in-Publication Data
Rounds, Glen, 1906–
Three billy goats Gruff / retold and illustrated
by Glen Rounds. — 1st. ed.
p.   cm.
Summary: Retells the folktale about three billy goats
who trick a troll that lives under a bridge.
ISBN 0-8234-1015-3
[1. Fairy tales. 2. Folklore—Norway.]   I. Asbjørnsen,
Peter Christen, 1812–1885. Tre bukkene Bruse. II. Title.
III. Title: 3 billy goats Gruff.
PZ8.R775Th   1993   92-23951   CIP   AC
398.24'5297358'09481—dc20
[E]

ISBN 0-8234-1136-2 (pbk.)

THREE BILLY GOATS GRUFF

retold and illustrated by
Glen Rounds

Holiday House/New York

Once on a time, there were three billy goats.

One was very small, one was middle-sized, and one was very large.

They were all named GRUFF, so people simply called them

THE THREE BILLY GOATS GRUFF.

On a certain morning, the Three Billy Goats Gruff were on their way to a distant hillside where the grass was especially tall and green and tender.

But to get to the hillside, they had to cross a bridge over a DEEP, SWIFT RIVER.

AND UNDER THAT BRIDGE LIVED A
GREAT, BIG, UGLY TROLL!

The smallest Billy Goat Gruff had just started across the bridge, trip-trap, trip-trap, trip-trap, when the troll roared from below,

"WHO'S THAT TRIPPING ACROSS MY BRIDGE?"

"It's only me, the smallest Billy Goat Gruff," the little billy goat answered in his tiny voice. "I'm going over to yonder hillside where the grass is so tall and green and tender."

"NO, YOU'RE NOT," roared the troll, "BECAUSE I'M GOING TO EAT YOU UP!"

"Oh, no!" cried the billy goat, "please don't eat me up! I'm much too small to make a meal for you! Wait for the second Billy Goat Gruff—he's MUCH bigger than I am!"

"Well, maybe you're right," growled the troll, "so be off with you!"

And he went back down under the bridge while the little billy goat ran to the green hillside beyond.

Then the second Billy Goat Gruff started
across the bridge,

trip-trap, trip-trap, trip-trap,
and again the troll roared,

"WHO'S TRIPPING ACROSS MY BRIDGE?"

"It's me, the second Billy Goat Gruff. But please don't eat me. The biggest Billy Goat Gruff is right behind me, and he is MUCH bigger!"

"Well," growled the troll, "get on with you. I'll wait for the big one!"

So the second billy goat ran safely across the bridge and to the green hillside beyond.

Then the BIGGEST billy goat stamped onto the bridge,

trip-trap, trip-trap, trip-trap!

And again the troll roared in his loudest voice,

"WHO'S THAT TRAMPING OVER MY BRIDGE?"

"It's me, the BIGGEST BILLY GOAT GRUFF!" shouted the billy goat in a voice almost as loud as the troll's.

"WHOEVER YOU ARE, I'M GOING TO EAT YOU UP RIGHT NOW!" roared the troll.

AND HE CLIMBED ONTO THE TOP OF THE BRIDGE.

"Well, come on then!" cried the big billy goat. "I've got sharp horns to butt you with! And hard hooves to trample you with!"

THAT'S WHAT THE BIG BILLY GOAT SAID.

THEN THE BIG BILLY GOAT
RAN AT THE TROLL

AND THE TROLL RAN AT
THE BILLY GOAT!

The big billy goat butted the ugly troll with his hard horns and trampled him with his sharp hooves.

Then he butted him again and knocked him off the bridge and into the DEEP, SWIFT RIVER BELOW.

The big billy goat stomped on across the bridge and onto the hillside where the grass was so tall and green and tender.

The great ugly troll was never seen again, and if the three Billy Goats Gruff haven't gone away, they are still on that hillside, getting fatter every day.

And now, as Grandmother used to say,

"Snip! Snap! Snout!
This tale's told out!"

Back in Alice's room, the book felt sublime in its always-and-forever home. Carefully, Alice repaired the girl's torn dress with some tape and read the story out loud.

"I don't mind at all that *this* one is missing," she said, reaching the very last page. "I know just what it says. 'And they lived happily ever after,' of course."

And then . . . the book found itself in Alice's hands once again. "I knew I'd find you!" Alice cried, gently touching the frayed yellow ribbon.

"Oh, Alice, I've been hoping you'd come!" said the librarian. "The book has been waiting for you. Please, take it for free.

"You know," she added, gazing at the book's cover, with its little girl and enchanted toadstool, "it was my favorite book too when I was young."

It wasn't long before the book heard a familiar voice. "I know it's here, I just know it is. I promise I'll hurry," the voice said breathlessly to the librarian.

"Okay, sweetheart, because we have to get the books out of the rain," the librarian answered.

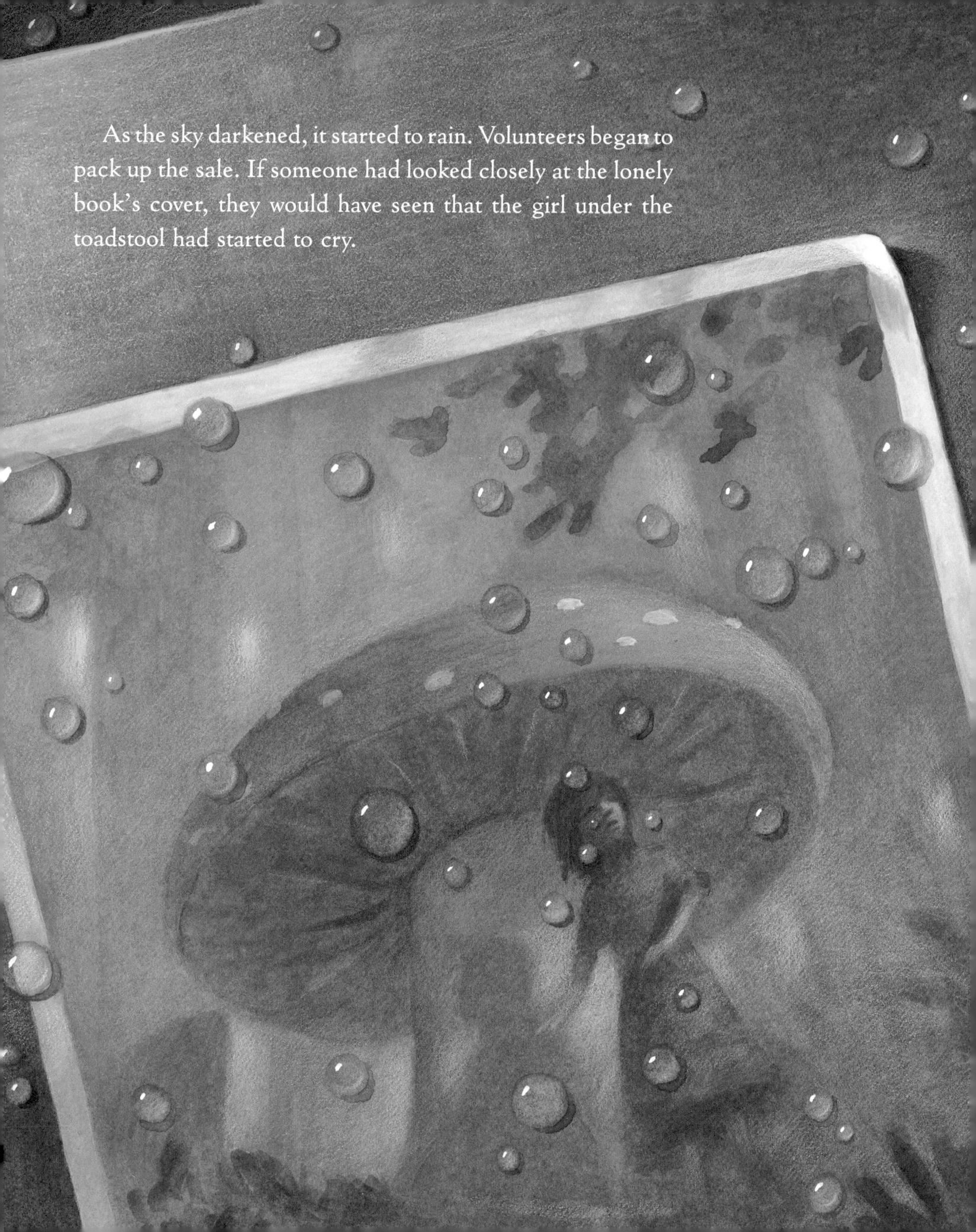

As the sky darkened, it started to rain. Volunteers began to pack up the sale. If someone had looked closely at the lonely book's cover, they would have seen that the girl under the toadstool had started to cry.

Then came a day that the book would remember forever. One morning, it found itself being carried upstairs and placed in the shade of a tree.

The book enjoyed the fresh air. All day long people peered down at it with kind faces, and many children picked it up and turned its pages. Other books were taken away, tucked under people's arms— good books about all sorts of good things, such as faraway planets and talking dogs. Still, none was quite as magical as the lonely book. Neither was any as ruined, which might have been why no one took the lonely book home.

Over time, Alice forgot about the book. Though she never really stopped loving it, it was replaced in her thoughts by other books, like a particularly sweet one about a sea horse and her sea home, and another mysterious one about ice, snow, and glass.

Meanwhile, at the library, volunteers occasionally came down to the basement to tend to the books or bring them new companions. Sometimes a volunteer would pick the lonely book up, leaf through its pages, and smile, remembering its marvelous toadstool. But the volunteer always put it back down with a sigh and left it behind.

The book grew lonelier and lonelier.

And the lonely book missed Alice.
Though all the books were kept tidy
and safe in the basement, it was very
dark. The book was lonelier than it
had ever been.

The following Saturday, Alice rushed back to the children's section, but the faded green book wasn't there. The librarian looked and looked for it, but she couldn't find it either. (A hardworking library volunteer had picked it up and, thinking it was meant for the Book Sale, taken it down to the basement. There the lonely book sat, patiently waiting for something to happen.)

Alice found a lot of other books to borrow, but they weren't the same. Saturday after Saturday she looked, but her book was never there. Alice missed it terribly.

But as soon as Alice arrived home, she remembered. "Daddy!" she cried. "I left my book at the library. Please can we go back and get it?"

"I'm sorry, Alice," her father replied. "The library is closed now, and I have to work all week. I promise I'll take you back next Saturday morning. I'm sure your friend the book will be there."

The next week at the library, there was a special event. A princess and a lion greeted Alice and all the children when they arrived and then ushered them into the Listening Room for a wonderful story about a princess and a lion.

After the event, Alice selected the princess and lion storybook to check out. In her excitement, she forgot all about renewing the old book about the girl in the forest.

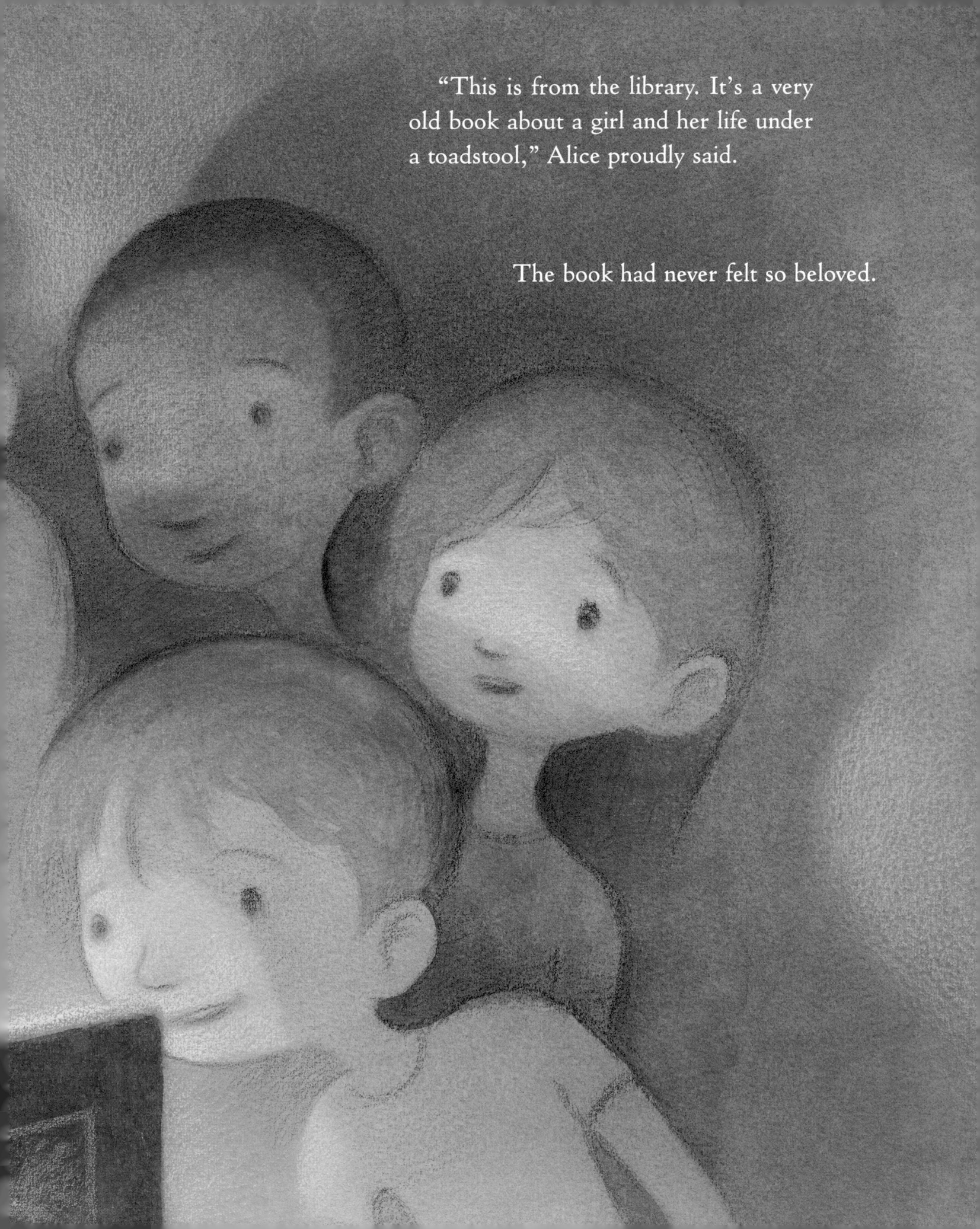

"This is from the library. It's a very old book about a girl and her life under a toadstool," Alice proudly said.

The book had never felt so beloved.

When she went to school every morning, Alice
gently tucked the book into her bag. One day, the
book was even featured at show-and-tell.

and then after her light was turned out she would read it herself by the light of the moon.

On the last, missing page she always imagined a happy ending and some fairies dancing with the girl around the toadstool.

Now Alice slept with the green book under her pillow, the better to dream about it.

When the book saw Alice's room—and the shelf where it would sleep, alongside so many familiar books from the library and some new books it had never met—it was very happy.

For six nights in a row, Alice's father read her the book at bedtime,

The next morning, a little girl sat reading in the corner of the library where the book sadly slept. She felt it under the leg of her rocking chair, leaned down, and picked it up. Turning its pages, she sighed.

"Daddy!" she whispered, and walked across to the fairy-tale section. "This is the most beautiful book I've ever read. Can I take it home?"

"I don't know, Alice," her father answered, reading a gigantic book almost bigger than himself. "It seems very fragile. And you already have so many books in your basket."

But Alice put three new books back and so was able to take the lonely book home, promising to be very careful with it.

Then, one very bad night, the book found itself completely forgotten, dropped in a dark corner by a daydreaming child, and not even the librarian found it.

Years and years passed, and after a while it seemed that only rarely would the book be checked out. Its cover was faded and on one page the girl's brown patchwork dress was torn. The last page of the book was missing.

More years passed, and now hardly ever would a child take the shabby book off the shelf. But it was still read with joy from time to time, and despite the book's worn appearance, its girl, toadstool, and story would always be enchanting.

The book became lonely.

As is the custom in libraries, after a time the book was moved to the children's section, along with other well-loved books that were no longer new. But the book was still taken home often, and so it was still happy.

Once there was a brand-new book that arrived at the library. It was green with a yellow ribbon inside to mark its pages. On its cover was a picture of a girl in the forest under a toadstool. The book found itself in the front of the library where the newest books were always placed.

The library was busy every day with children looking for books about everything in the world, and the moss-green book about the girl in the forest was often chosen and taken home.

Whenever the book was returned, it was placed back on the shelf where the newest books lived. There was a long list of children waiting for the book, and it hardly ever slept at the library.

The Lonely Book

Kate Bernheimer

illustrated by

Chris Sheban

schwartz wade books • new york

For Xia and her cousins—who all love to read. —K.B.

For Ron, whom I miss. —C.S.

Text copyright © 2012 by Kate Bernheimer
Illustrations copyright © 2012 by Chris Sheban
All rights reserved. Published in the United States by Schwartz & Wade Books,
an imprint of Random House Children's Books, a division of
Random House, Inc., New York.
Schwartz & Wade Books and the colophon are trademarks of
Random House, Inc.
Visit us on the Web! www.randomhouse.com/kids
Educators and librarians, for a variety of teaching tools, visit us at
www.randomhouse.com/teachers
Library of Congress Cataloging-in-Publication Data
Bernheimer, Kate.
The lonely book / Kate Bernheimer ; [illustrated by Chris Sheban].—1st ed.
p. cm.
Summary: Once popular, a library book becomes lonely as it grows shabbier
until a young girl rediscovers it, but when it becomes lost again they both
wonder if they will have a happy ending.
ISBN 978-0-375-86226-7 (trade) — ISBN 978-0-375-96226-4 (glb)
[1. Books and reading—Fiction. 2. Libraries—Fiction. 3. Loneliness—Fiction.]
I. Sheban, Chris, ill. II. Title.
PZ7.B45566Lon 2011
[E]—dc22
2010005283
The text of this book is set in Cg Cloister.
The illustrations were rendered in watercolor, graphite,
and colored pencil on paper.
MANUFACTURED IN CHINA
10 9 8 7 6 5 4 3 2 1
First Edition

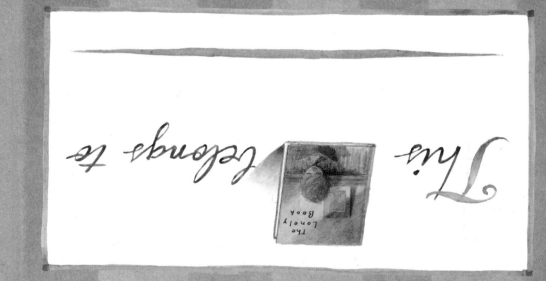